j398.21 Jacobs, Joseph,
J          1854-1916.

        Tattercoats


   $14.95

| DATE | | | |
|---|---|---|---|
| | | | |
| | | | |
| | | | |
| | | | |
| | | | |
| | | | |
| | | | |
| | | | |
| | | | |
| | | | |
| | | | |
| | | | |
| | | | |

# TATTERCOATS

# Tattercoats

COLLECTED AND EDITED BY
## JOSEPH JACOBS

ILLUSTRATED BY
## MARGOT TOMES

G. P. Putnam's Sons   New York

Copyright © 1989 by Margot Tomes. All rights reserved.
This book, or parts thereof, may not be reproduced in any
form without permission in writing from the publishers.
Published simultaneously in Canada.
Printed in Hong Kong by South China Printing Co.
Designed by Golda Laurens
Library of Congress Cataloging-in-Publication Data
Jacobs, Joseph, 1854–1916. Tattercoats/collected and edited
by Joseph Jacobs; illustrated by Margot Tomes.  p.   cm.
Summary: Retells the traditional English tale of how
poor, neglected Tattercoats comes to marry the Prince.
[1. Fairy tales.  2. Folklore — England.]  I. Tomes, Margot, ill.  II.Title.
PZ8.J19Tat 1989 389.2'1'0942 — dc19 [E] 88-2357 CIP AC
ISBN 0-399-21584-0
First impression

To Refna
— M.T.

In a great Palace by the sea there once dwelt a very rich old lord, who had neither wife nor children living, only one little grand-daughter, whose face he had never seen in all her life. He hated her bitterly, because at her birth his favorite daughter died; and when the old nurse brought him the baby, he swore that it might live or die as it liked, but he would never look on its face as long as it lived.

So he turned his back, and sat by his window looking out over the sea, and weeping great tears for his lost daughter, till his white hair and beard grew down over his shoulders and twined round his chair and crept into the chinks of the floor, and his tears, dropping on to the window ledge, wore a channel through the stone, and ran away in a little river to the great sea.

And, meanwhile, his granddaughter grew up with no one to care for her, or clothe her; only the old nurse, when no one was by, would sometimes give her a dish of scraps from the kitchen, or a torn petticoat from the ragbag; while the other servants of the Palace would drive her from the house with blows and mocking words, calling her "Tattercoats," and pointing at her bare feet and shoulders, till she ran away crying, to hide among the bushes.

And so she grew up, with little to eat or wear, spending her days in the fields and lanes, with only the gooseherd for a companion, who would play to her so merrily on his little pipe, when she was hungry, or cold, or tired, that she forgot all her troubles, and fell to dancing, with his flock of noisy geese for partners.

But, one day, people told each other that the King was traveling through the land, and in the town nearby was to give a great ball, to all the lords and ladies of the country, when the Prince, his only son, was to choose a wife.

One of the royal invitations was brought to the Palace by the sea, and the servants carried it up to the old lord, who still sat by his window, wrapped in his long white hair and weeping into the little river that was fed by his tears.

But when he heard the King's command, he dried his eyes and bade them bring shears to cut him loose, for his hair had bound him a fast prisoner and he could not move. And then he sent them for rich clothes, and jewels, which he put on; and he ordered them to saddle the white horse, with gold and silk, that he might ride to meet the King.

Meanwhile Tattercoats had heard of the great doings in the town, and she sat by the kitchen door weeping because she could not go to see them. And when the old nurse heard her crying she went to the Lord of the Palace, and begged him to take his granddaughter with him to the King's ball.

But he only frowned and told her to be silent, while the servants laughed and said : "Tattercoats is happy in her rags, playing with the gooseherd, let her be—it is all she is fit for."

A second, and then a third time, the old nurse begged him to let the girl go with him, but she was answered only by black looks and fierce words, till she was driven from the room by the jeering servants, with blows and mocking words.

Weeping over her ill-success, the old nurse went to look for Tattercoats; but the girl had been turned from the door by the cook, and had run away to tell her friend the gooseherd how unhappy she was because she could not go to the King's ball.

But when the gooseherd had listened to her story, he bade her cheer up, and proposed that they should go together into the town to see the King, and all the fine things; and when she looked sorrowfully down at her rags and bare feet, he played a note or two upon his pipe, so gay and merry, that she forgot all about her tears and her troubles, and before she well knew, the herdboy had taken her by the hand and she, and he, and the geese before them, were dancing down the road toward the town.

Before they had gone very far, a handsome young man, splendidly dressed, rode up and stopped to ask the way to the castle where the King was staying; and when he found that they too were going thither, he got off his horse and walked beside them along the road.

The herdboy pulled out his pipe and played a low sweet tune, and the stranger looked again and again at Tattercoats' lovely face till he fell deeply in love with her, and begged her to marry him.

But she only laughed, and shook her golden head.

"You would be finely put to shame if you had a goosegirl for your wife!" said she; "go and ask one of the great ladies you will see tonight at the King's ball, and do not flout poor Tattercoats."

But the more she refused him the sweeter the pipe played, and the deeper the young man fell in love; till at last he begged her, as a proof of his sincerity, to come that night at twelve to the King's ball, just as she was, with the herdboy and his geese, and in her torn petticoat and bare feet, and he would dance with her before the King and the lords and ladies, and present her to them all, as his dear and honored bride.

So when night came, and the hall in the castle was full of light and music, and the lords and ladies were dancing before the King, just as the clock struck twelve, Tattercoats and the herdboy, followed by his flock of noisy geese, entered at the great doors, and walked straight up the ballroom, while on either side the ladies whispered, the lords laughed, and the King seated at the far end stared in amazement.

But as they came in front of the throne, Tattercoats' lover rose from beside the King, and came to meet her. Taking her by the hand, he kissed her thrice before them all, and turned to the King.

"Father!" he said, for it was the Prince himself, "I have made my choice, and here is my bride, the loveliest girl in all the land, and the sweetest as well!"

Before he had finished speaking, the herdboy put his pipe to his lips and played a few low notes that sounded like a bird singing far off in the woods; and as he played, Tattercoats' rags were changed to shining robes sewn with glittering jewels, a golden crown lay upon her golden hair, and the flock of geese behind her became a crowd of dainty pages, bearing her long train.

And as the King rose to greet her as his daughter, the trumpets sounded loudly in honor of the new Princess, and the people outside in the street said to each other:

"Ah! now the Prince has chosen for his wife the loveliest girl in all the land!"

But the gooseherd was never seen again, and no one knew what became of him; while the old lord went home once more to his Palace by the sea, for he could not stay at Court, when he had sworn never to look on his granddaughter's face.

So there he still sits by his window, if you could only see him, as you some day may, weeping more bitterly than ever, as he looks out over the sea.

## JOSEPH JACOBS

Joseph Jacobs was born in Australia in 1854. After living in England for many years, he moved to the United States in 1900. He was a writer, folklorist and historian who specialized in Jewish history, and he taught at the Jewish Theological Seminary in New York. Besides editing the *American Hebrew*, he was the editor of *Folk-Lore*, the journal of the Folk-Lore Society, and he compiled several collections of folktales, from one of which *Tattercoats* is taken. Joseph Jacobs died in 1916.

## MARGOT TOMES

Margot Tomes grew up in a rural Long Island town. She graduated from Pratt Institute and worked for many years as a textile designer before turning to illustrating children's books. Her elegant illustrations have appeared in more than fifty books, among them works by Jean Fritz, Tony Johnston and Wanda Gág. Margot Tomes lives in New York City.